W9-CGL-510

PETER PIPER'S
Practical Principles
of Plain & Perfect Pronunciation

PETER PIPER'S
Practical Principles
of Plain & Perfect Pronunciation

DOVER PUBLICATIONS, INC.
NEW YORK

Published in Canada by General Publishing Company, Ltd., 30 Lesmill Road, Don Mills, Toronto, Ontario.

This Dover edition, first published in 1970, is an unabridged and unaltered republication of the work published by LeRoy Phillips in Boston in 1911. The 1911 edition reproduced woodcuts of the first American edition, published by Carter Andrews and Company, Lancaster, Massachusetts, in 1830, a copy of which was in the Lancaster Town Library. For further details, see Prefatory Note.

International Standard Book Number

(paper): 0-486-22560-7 (cloth): 0-486-22660-3

Library of Congress Catalog Card Number: 75-106941

Manufactured in the United States of America
Dover Publications, Inc.
180 Varick Street
New York, N.Y. 10014

Prefatory Note

The original publisher of these alliterative jingles was J. Harris, successor to E. Newbery of St. Paul's Churchyard, London. In the early years of the Nineteenth Century he issued many juvenile favorites, some old and others new, in a series known as "Harris's Cabinet." This rhymed advertisement at some time appeared with his books and suggests the verses of modern bards of business:

At Harris's, St. Paul's Church-yard,
Good children meet a sure reward;
In coming home the other day
I heard a little master say,
For every penny there he took
He had received a little book,

With covers neat, and cuts so pretty,
There's not its like in all the city;
And that for two-pence he could buy
A story-book would make one cry;
For little more a book of riddles:
Then let us not buy drums or fiddles,
Nor yet be stopt at pastry-cooks,
But spend our money all in books;
For when we've learnt each book by
  heart
Mamma will treat us with a tart.

"Peter Piper" was first published in America about 1830 by Carter Andrews and Company at Lancaster, Massachusetts. The quaint illustrations for the present issue were taken directly from the copy of this now scarce edition in the possession of the Lancaster Town Library.

The purpose of Carter Andrews and Company in America must have been similar to that of Newbery and Harris in England, for many of the toy books of the period bear their imprint. The American publishers, however, introduced some local color. On the back covers appeared a front view of that characteristic work by Bulfinch, the brick meeting house of the First Church of Lancaster, encircled by the words "Lancaster Cabinet of Amusement and Instruction," and the engraver, in "Figuring Francis Fribble on a Frenchman's Filly" in the present book, has included a milestone marked "Bolton (a neighboring town to Lancaster) 4 M."

"Peter Piper" has recently appeared with the imprint of the Scott-Thaw Company, New York, but the illustrations do not attempt to reproduce the quaint character of the wood cuts which adorned the pages of the Lancaster Edition.

Some of these jingles are occasionally discovered detached from their fellows, but must be traced to " Peter Piper " as their source. An instance of this is a little book entitled "Tongue Twisters," published by the Carol Press of Boston.

The compiler of these notes is informed by Mr. Davis L. James, of Cincinnati, of an instance, a generation back, where, although the printed book and the illustrations were unknown, yet the jingles were a family possession, the children being taught them orally as a means of acquiring the " Practical Principles of Plain and Perfect Pronunciation."

LeRoy Phillips

Preface

PETER PIPER, without Pretension to Precocity or Profoundness, Puts Pen to Paper to Produce these Puzzling Pages, Purposely to Please the Palates of Pretty Prattling Playfellows, Proudly Presuming that with Proper Penetration it will Probably, and Perhaps Positively, Prove a Peculiarly Pleasant and Profitable Path to Proper, Plain, and Precise Pronunciation.

He Prays Parents to Purchase this Playful Performance, Partly to Pay him for his Patience and Pains; Partly to Provide for the Profit of the Printers and Publishers; but Principally to Prevent the Pernicious Prevalence of Perverse Pronunciation.

PETER PIPER'S
Practical Principles
of Plain & Perfect Pronunciation

A a

Andrew Airpump ask'd his Aunt her Ail-
ment:
Did Andrew Airpump ask his Aunt her
Ailment?
If Andrew Airpump ask'd his Aunt her
Ailment,
Where was the Ailment of Andrew Air-
pump's Aunt?

B b

Billy Button bought a Butter'd Biscuit:
Did Billy Button buy a Butter'd Biscuit?
If Billy Button bought a Butter'd Biscuit,
Where's the Butter'd Biscuit Billy Button
    bought?

C c

Captain Crackskull crack'd a Catchpoll's
  Cockscomb :
Did Captain Crackskull crack a Catch-
  poll's Cockscomb ?
If Captain Crackskull crack'd a Catch-
  poll's Cockscomb,
Where's the Catchpoll's Cockscomb Cap-
  tain Crackskull crack'd ?

D d

Davy Dolldrum dream'd he drove a Dragon:
Did Davy Dolldrum dream he drove a Dragon?
If Davy Dolldrum dream'd he drove a Dragon,
Where's the Dragon Davy Dolldrum dream'd he drove?

E e

Enoch Elkrig ate an empty Eggshell:
Did Enoch Elkrig eat an empty Eggshell?
If Enoch Elkrig ate an empty Eggshell,
Where's the empty Eggshell Enoch Elk-
   rig ate?

F f

Francis Fribble figured on a Frenchman's
    Filly:
Did Francis Fribble figure on a French-
    man's Filly?
If Francis Fribble figured on a French-
    man's Filly,
Where's the Frenchman's Filly Francis
    Fribble figured on?

G g

Gaffer Gilpin grabbed a Goose and Gan-
der:
Did Gaffer Gilpin grab a Goose and Gan-
der?
If Gaffer Gilpin grabbed a Goose and Gan-
der,
Where's the Goose and Gander Gaffer
Gilpin grabbed?

H h

Humphrey Hunchback had a Hundred
    Hedgehogs:
Did Humphrey Hunchback have a Hun-
    dred Hedgehogs?
If Humphrey Hunchback had a Hundred
    Hedgehogs,
Where's the Hundred Hedgehogs Hum-
    phrey Hunchback had?

I i

Inigo Impey itched for an Indian Image:
Did Inigo Impey itch for an Indian Image?
If Inigo Impey itched for an Indian Image,
Where's the Indian Image Inigo Impey
itched for?

J j

Jumping Jackey jeer'd a Jesting Juggler:
Did Jumping Jackey jeer a Jesting Jug-
    gler?
If Jumping Jackey jeer'd a Jesting Juggler,
Where's the Jesting Juggler Jumping
    Jackey jeered?

K k

Kimbo Kemble kick'd his Kinsman's Kettle:

Did Kimbo Kemble kick his Kinsman's
Kettle?

If Kimbo Kemble kick'd his Kinsman's
Kettle,

Where's the Kinsman's Kettle Kimbo
Kemble kick'd?

L l

Lanky Lawrence lost his Lass and Lobster:
Did Lanky Lawrence lose his Lass and
    Lobster?
If Lanky Lawrence lost his Lass and Lob-
    ster?
Where are the Lass and Lobster Lanky
    Lawrence lost?

M m

Matthew Mendlegs miss'd a meddling
  Monkey:
Did Matthew Mendlegs miss a meddling
  Monkey?
If Matthew Mendlegs miss'd a meddling
  Monkey,
Where's the meddling Monkey Matthew
  Mendlegs miss'd?

N n

Neddie Noodle nipp'd his Neighbor's Nutmegs:

Did Neddie Noodle nip his Neighbor's Nutmegs?

If Neddie Noodle nipped his Neighbor's Nutmegs,

Where are the Neighbor's Nutmegs Neddie Noodle nipp'd?

O o

Oliver Oglethorpe ogled an Owl and
    Oyster :
Did Oliver Oglethorpe ogle an Owl and
    Oyster ?
If Oliver Oglethorpe ogled an Owl and
    Oyster,
Where are the Owl and Oyster Oliver
    Oglethorpe ogled ?

P p

Peter Piper pick'd a Peck of Pickled
    Peppers:
Did Peter Piper pick a Peck of Pickled
    Peppers?
If Peter Piper pick'd a peck of Pickled
    Peppers,
Where's the Peck of Pickled Peppers
    Peter Piper pick'd?

Q q

Quixote Quicksight quiz'd a queerish
Quidbox:
Did Quixote Quicksight quiz a queerish
Quidbox?
If Quixote Quicksight quiz'd a queerish
Quidbox,
Where's the queerish Quidbox Quixote
Quicksight quiz'd?

R r

Rory Rumpus rode a rawboned Racer:
Did Rory Rumpus ride a rawboned Racer?
If Rory Rumpus rode a rawboned Racer,
Where's the rawboned Racer Rory Rumpus
    rode?

S s

Sammy Smellie smelt a Smell of Small-
   coal:
Did Sammy Smellie smell a Smell of
   Smallcoal?
If Sammy Smellie smelt a Smell of Small-
   coal,
Where's the Smell of Smallcoal Sammy
   Smellie smelt?

T t

Tip-Toe Tommy turn'd a Turk for Two-
pence:
Did Tip-Toe Tommy turn a Turk for
Two-pence?
If Tip-Toe Tommy turn'd a Turk for
Two-pence,
Where's the Turk for Two-pence Tip-Toe
Tommy turn'd?

U u

Uncle's Usher urg'd an ugly Urchin:
Did Uncle's Usher urge an ugly Urchin?
If Uncle's Usher urg'd an ugly Urchin,
Where's the ugly Urchin Uncle's Usher
    urg'd?

V v

Villiam Veedon vip'd his Vig and Vaist-
   coat :
Did Villiam Veedon vipe his Vig and
   Vaistcoat ?
If Villiam Veedon vip'd his Vig and Vaist-
   coat
Where are the Vig and Vaistcoat Villiam
   Veedon vip'd ?

W w

Walter Waddle won a walking Wager :
Did Walter Waddle win a walking Wager?
If Walter Waddle won a walking Wager,
Where's the walking Wager Walter
    Waddle Won?

X x Y y Z z

X Y Z have made my Brains to crack-o,
X smokes, Y snuffs, and Z chews tobacco;
Yet oft by X Y Z much learning's taught;
But Peter Piper beats them all to naught.